A BORN PROVIDER

AN M/M KINK ROMANCE

THE LACTIN BROTHERHOOD
BOOK TWO

ALEX BLAINE

IN INK PRESS

In Ink Press (a division of Surrendered Press)

A Born Provider

Copyright © 2024 by Alex Blaine

All rights reserved.

No part of this book may be reproduced in any form or by any electronic or mechanical means, including information storage and retrieval systems, without written permission from the author, except for the use of brief quotations in a book review.

CONTENTS

1. Chad — 1
2. Ricky — 9
3. Chad — 23
4. Ricky — 33
5. Chad — 41
6. Chad — 51
7. Ricky — 57
8. Chad — 65
9. Ricky — 73
10. Chad — 79
11. Ricky — 87
12. Chad — 93
13. Ricky — 101
14. Chad — 107
15. Ricky — 115

1

CHAD

I was working out with Cory when I remembered the inquiry I got from my website. Since he was involved in the kink community too, I figured he was a good person to ask about it. "Hey, have you been to Lashes and Lace?"

"Yeah, a few times. It's a nice set-up." He grunted through his set before stopping for a breath. "It's still kinda new, but the membership is growing pretty fast. They do a lot of theme nights that draw in guests from all over the state."

That sounded interesting. "They contacted me about doing an event there. A Little Play Night. They want me there for a feeding. What do you think?"

He grinned and then glanced down at my chest, as pretty much everyone did whenever we talked about my unusual gift.

And I truly believed it was a gift. Although five percent of the male population had started consistently lactating over the past twenty years, it was still not broadly discussed outside of those circles, so I felt lucky to be one of the chosen ones.

I was also one of the few in that population who had zero qualms about it.

Since the first time I noticed milk leaking out of my chest when I was in high school, I thought it was pretty fucking awesome. Most of my boyfriends did too... At least, at first. Eventually, the novelty and inconvenience wore off.

Which was why I didn't really do the dating thing much anymore.

My job was too hectic for anything serious, and when I needed to scratch an itch, there was always a line of milk sluts ready to show up for a quick booty call... Or nippy call, as it were.

"Yeah, you should do it." Cory shrugged. "It'd be a great way to meet new clients and probably make some decent money. It's an upscale place with a ridiculously high buy-in, so I would think they'd pay well."

"Yeah, two grand for the night. I'm guessing it'll be two or three hours… Depending on how many Littles are interested in partaking."

"Oh, they'll all want a taste." He looked up at me and winked. "What night is it? Maybe I'll show up too. I've always kinda wondered what it tastes like."

I finished the set of curls I was doing and put down the weight. "The message I received sounded like it was Littles only, so I doubt you'd be welcomed. But you know how to reach me." I winked. "I'll give you the friends-and-family discount."

He started up his next set and kept his gaze on the ground in front of him, suddenly not making eye contact with me. "Yeah, I might just do that."

Whatever. Everybody wanted to taste it at least once. Some people were really into it, others just appreciated the novelty and the ability to say they tried it. As long as they paid me, I didn't care what their intentions were. I worked with men, women, medical facilities, and tons of gyms. My milk was just a means to an end.

Besides, when I was getting paid for it, there was no sex involved. It was just business.

Of course, when I was hooking up with someone, either paid or unpaid, there was usually some degree of suckling involved. Mostly because I leaked like a fucking faucet once I got aroused.

At least, that was how it used to be.

These days, I was either losing my sex drive or getting bored of the business aspect of nursing, because getting off was not as fun as it used to be. Lately, the only time I got off was after I woke up to deal with my morning wood but not because I was super into it.

Maybe I'd never be into it again.

After our workout, I went into the break room and pumped, leaving a pint of fresh milk and another pint of frozen in their fridge for clients. Then, I picked up a sandwich for lunch and headed over to the hospital. My buddy, Dave, who worked as a pediatric pharmacist at the hospital asked me to come by. They wanted to contract me to come in twice a day for the next few weeks. A set of twins were born prematurely to an addict, and they needed "skin-to-skin contact." That was his code word for discreet nursing to help them put on some weight.

Those were my favorite jobs.

I loved not only cuddling those tiny babies and giving them the attention that their biological parents couldn't offer, but the fat and protein content in my milk was very high, making it an ideal supplement for an undernourished baby.

Everyone at the hospital knew me, so I grabbed my visitor pass from the front desk and headed up to the NICU.

"Chad, good to see you." Dave patted my shoulder and walked me to the room the twins were in. "Thank you for coming. These tiny little girls need to get some meat on their bones…" He turned and gave me a once-over glance. "And you look like you could use the cuddles."

I laughed and shook my head. "Always, and I'm happy to do it. I don't get nearly enough cuddles these days."

I said it as a joke, but we both knew there was more truth to it than I wanted to acknowledge.

He set me up in a gliding chair in the corner of a large room and rolled two incubators over to me. "They're surprisingly healthy, just small." He lifted the plastic lid from one of the bassinets and turned to me. "Do you want one at a time or both together?"

I had a big lunch and guzzled a bottle of electrolytes, so I knew I had plenty of milk available for their tiny little tummies. "Both is fine. Once I get them in place, we can just chill here for an hour or two. I don't have another appointment till tonight."

"Awesome. They need the time."

After I unbuttoned my shirt and wiped my skin with antiseptic wipes, Dave carefully detached the first baby from the monitors on her body and placed her up against me. Her little mouth immediately found my nipple and latched on as I curled her up in my arm.

We repeated the process with the other baby, and they were like two little footballs in my arms as he covered us up with a lightweight receiving blanket. "No one should bother you, but if anyone asks, just say you're the dad. Unfortunately, we don't expect any actual family members to come around for these two."

It was heartbreaking to know they might be alone in

this world, but at least I was able to do my small part. "We're fine. Go do what you need to do."

He nodded and took a step back. "I'll be back to check on you in about twenty minutes to see if you need anything."

I gently rocked the glider and closed my eyes. At least for a little while, I had what I needed.

A purpose.

2

RICKY

A Little night.

It sounded perfect. Exactly what I needed in order to start meeting people. At least, that was what Mark and Adam kept telling me.

They liked to take turns lecturing me over the fact that I'd never meet a Daddy in that boring office of mine. I knew they were right, but it was still scary to put myself out there in such a public way.

I'd been to a couple of munches with them that Lashes and Lace had put on. They were all casual and fun. Well, fun if you liked talking to people. I didn't, but I could appreciate watching everybody else talk and interact… And they seemed to be having fun, so it wasn't all bad.

But an event at their club sounded like a bigger commitment. Not only would I be expected to dress the part of a Little, which I'd never done publicly, but I would also have to allow myself to regress in a way that made me completely vulnerable to those around me.

I wanted it so bad, but I was also afraid to be taken advantage of. Again.

The last time I let someone really see that side of me ended in disaster. Okay, it wasn't a complete disaster, but it was a time filled with humiliation and shame that took me a long time to move past. That was two years ago, and I felt ready to try again. Maybe.

I turned back to my spreadsheet so I could focus on my work. I was working on a huge project that had a rushed deadline. As a forensic accountant, I loved these kinds of challenges. In this case, the owner of several local med spas had hired my firm to audit their books. They were convinced someone in the company was stealing, but they couldn't figure out where the problem was.

I'd only been digging through the files for two days, but I could already see where the discrepancies were starting to pop up. That was what I loved.

Math wasn't everybody's jam, but it was definitely mine. I loved that every problem had a solution. Numbers made sense, and if you knew how to manipulate them the right way, everything worked out as it was supposed to. If only people were as easy to understand.

Adam said I would have a better time with people if I weren't so damn shy. He was probably right. My shyness could be debilitating at the best of times, but that was why I needed to push myself out of my comfort zone. If it were up to me, I'd probably be completely nonverbal and communicate only through my computer for the rest of my life.

But deep down, I knew that wasn't the kind of life I wanted.

I wanted a partner. Someone who could push me when I was turning inward and support me when I needed downtime.

Someone to take care of me.

Before I chickened out, I picked up my phone and texted Adam and Mark back. ***I'll go. But I'm not promising to participate.***

Mark responded back with a laughing emoji. *We won't force you to do anything, but I heard there's a surprise guest that everyone is gonna want to meet.*

Adam finally chimed in. *Who is it? I haven't heard anything about a surprise guest.*

Mark responded back with a string of emojis that I didn't even recognize. *It's a surprise. But you're gonna like it. And if you don't, more for me.*

More for you? I finally jumped into the conversation, curious what he meant by that. *Like a candy bar or cupcakes?* I loved cupcakes.

Kinda...But not exactly. You'll find out when you get there.

Great, now there was even more pressure to participate in something special. I hated being put on the spot and expected to love something when maybe I wouldn't love it. Or maybe I would love it but be too embarrassed to participate.

God, I hoped it wasn't some sort of person dressed up in a big animal costume. Those were fun to look at, but I never wanted to sit on their lap or take a picture with them. Especially not if I was wearing the one-piece pajamas I kept tucked in the back of my drawer for those times when I needed to be Little. I didn't get to wear them often, but I could be brave and pretend I was going to a Halloween party and everyone would be dressed up.

That might be the only way Adam and Mark could get me out of my house.

I stood in the changing room with my arms crossed over my chest, trying to hide even though there was no way that was possible. "I feel so silly."

"That's the point." Adam was wearing a cropped T-shirt and short shorts with a diaper poking out the top of his waistband. "We're gonna be silly tonight."

Mark was in one-piece pajamas, similar to mine, but with built-in feet instead of cuffed at the ankles. "You're allowed to be yourself here, remember? Don't worry about anybody else. Just let Little Ricky come out and play with us and have some fun. You need this, man, more than any of us."

"Yeah, I guess you're right." I dropped my arms to my sides and shook out my shoulders. "Okay, I'm ready."

Adam grabbed my shoulder and then wrapped his arm around me. "Let's do this."

There was a door from the changing room that went directly into the Littles playroom, so at least I didn't have to walk down any halls where other people might see me.

That was the good part.

The bad part was that as soon as we walked into the playroom, all eyes were on us.

Mark and Adam both loved attention, so they were happy to take the lead, smiling and waving to their onlookers while dragging me behind them.

I kept my eyes down on the ground in front of me, not wanting to acknowledge that anyone could even see me. I hated when people looked at me. Luckily, the attention quickly fell away from us and everyone went back to what they were doing while we headed straight to the snack table.

"There is a candy bar!" I grabbed the big scoop in the jellybean jar and took a small amount out, then placed them on a plate. "I love jellybeans."

"And cotton candy." Adam already had a blue sticky

mess on his face, but he was wearing the biggest grin I'd ever seen on him. "It's so good."

I laughed and reached for a chocolate truffle. I loved chocolate. And if I was gonna indulge tonight, I was going all in. At least as far as treats were concerned.

"Apple, grape, or milk?" Mark was standing by the drink table.

I looked at him, wondering why he even had to ask. He knew what I liked. "Milk. Definitely milk."

He grabbed two cartons. "White or chocolate?"

As if. "White, obviously." I once saw a documentary on how they made chocolate milk for packaging, and…it kinda ruined it for me. I liked making chocolate milk at home or when I knew it was made from white milk and chocolate, but not the kind that came premixed in a carton.

He handed me a tiny carton with a straw attached and grabbed one for himself.

"Thank you, Marky."

"I want to color." Adam pointed at one of the empty tables.

"Me too." Mark was right behind him.

Since my friends had spotted their first activity, I followed along behind, doing my best to subtly look around at all the people and toys spread throughout the room. About ten Daddies and caretakers were scattered along the outer walls, watching their Littles from a distance. I couldn't press down the tinge of envy for the boys and girls who had somebody taking care of them.

I wanted a Daddy too.

We all sat on the floor in front of a coffee table and reached for coloring sheets. There was an assortment of crayons and markers in every shape and grip size. I chose colored pencils because they were the most consistent. If I wanted a dark line, I sharpened it. If I wanted a lighter line, I used a smooth tip. Like math, it was perfectly logical, and there was always a simple solution.

Dumb markers ran out of ink and dried up. Definitely not consistent.

I grabbed a picture of a penguin and a black pencil and began coloring. I hadn't even filled in the top of its head before Mark gasped. "There he is. Our milk Daddy."

A BORN PROVIDER

Adam and I both snapped our heads up to see what Mark was talking about. "Who? Where?"

Mark was staring over my shoulder at a man in the corner of a sofa. He was huge like a football player and started to unbutton his shirt.

I didn't understand why he would be there. "Is he a stripper?"

Mark bit his lip and shook his head. "Better. He makes milk."

Adam's jaw dropped, and he turned to look back at the man. "Really? Like milk Daddy as in…we can drink from him?"

"Yep. We can all take a turn."

They both glanced at me. "You're so doing this, Ricky."

I immediately began to shake my head, and I was pretty sure my lungs stopped working. "No way. I can't do that. That would be… I can't."

We all turned back and watched as a baby Little crawled over to the couch and was helped up by his Daddy to get in position on the man's lap.

Mark was practically drooling. "See, he's doing it.

That's why they brought him in tonight. He's our special surprise."

I couldn't look away as the Little, who was slightly smaller than me but a good ten years older, nestled up against the man's chest. It took a second, but then he seemed to be drinking from him the way a baby would from a mother. "I didn't even know that was possible."

"It is. There's a whole organization of guys who make milk. Milk brothers or something… I don't know the name, but this guy does it as a business. You can literally hire him to feed you." How did Mark know so much about this?

Well, that was interesting. I watched in amazement as the boy continued to drink for a few minutes before pulling off. He then gave the milkman a hug and crawled away with his Daddy. There was immediately a new boy on the couch and in the man's lap, just as eager to taste his offering.

"The line's getting long. I'm getting in it now. I don't want him to run out." Mark stood up and looked at us.

Adam looked back at the man in horror. "Will he run out?"

"Probably. I'm sure it's not an unlimited supply, and I really wanna taste him."

Adam stood up too, and they both turned to me. "You coming, Ricky?"

I got up and walked over to the line that had already formed, but mostly I was just watching. And trying to keep my dick hidden because it had gotten hard from thinking about tasting a real Daddy's milk.

Mark and Adam chatted amongst themselves, but I didn't pay attention to what they were saying. I just watched, stared really, as boys and girls and even a puppy climbed into his lap and got a taste.

My mouth was watering, but I was still unsure whether I could try it myself.

"Do you want to go first?" Adam asked Mark.

He nodded quickly. "Yeah, I won't take too much." Then he looked back at me and winked. "I'll make sure to leave you a few drops."

I swallowed as I saw my friend slip onto the couch, spread out, and latch on to the sexy man. I took a chance and looked up at his face and realized he was staring right back at me. *Oh my god. He knows I want to try it.*

Then again, he was probably thinking I looked silly in my sailor outfit. I liked boats, so sue me.

True to his word, Mark didn't spend too much time, and suddenly, it was Adam's turn. I watched in wonder as Adam took his position, and then I realized I would be next. No way. I couldn't do it. I grabbed a business card that was stacked on the coffee table and followed Mark back to where we'd been coloring.

He looked at me and frowned. "You don't want to try it?"

I shook my head, finally taking a deep breath. "Nah, I'm pretty full." I glanced at the carton of milk that suddenly seemed unappetizing. "How was it?"

Mark grinned. "Really good. Kinda like the milk that's left after you eat all your cereal."

I loved that milk.

"And it's warm. I was afraid I'd fall asleep if I stayed any longer."

"Yeah, that's what I thought."

Adam came back and dropped onto the floor beside me. "You should get back in line. It's really cool. I grabbed his card. I might need to hire him when I have a bad day or can't sleep."

My thoughts wandered to the card I'd slipped inside the wrist cuff of my pajamas.

But I wasn't gonna call him. Probably not, anyway. What would I even say?

3

CHAD

The Little night was more fun than I expected.

They were all so cute and sweet as they tentatively climbed onto my lap and figured out how to latch on. It was always an adjustment the first time, especially for those who'd never tried it before. But even if they'd experienced suckling without milk, when those first few drops begin to flow, there was always a bit of surprise and excitement until they got into a rhythm.

A few of them had to be nudged away by their caretakers when they got a little greedy, but most were happy with a minute or two of feeding before going back to the person that they'd arrived with. Except for the cute little sailor boy who had been watching me all night.

When he got out of line, I was disappointed.

I could tell how badly he wanted to try to suckle, but he was obviously shy. Very shy. In fact, on the few instances I was able to make eye contact with him, he immediately turned away, as if he could make himself invisible.

But I did notice that he took my card.

I didn't have high expectations that he'd use it, but if he did, I would do my best to talk him into a personal session. Not everyone wanted to suckle. Some Littles preferred a bottle or sippy cup so they could be in their space with their people. But I was hopeful he'd be willing to give it a try so I could possibly get to know him a bit.

I'd worked with plenty of first-timers who warred between shame and self-consciousness about wanting to drink straight from the tap. It was obviously not a common situation, but for those who needed the milk proteins that only human milk could provide, it was the best method of delivery.

Also, the most expensive.

Which was good for me but bad for customers who were cost conscious. Although, I had options for everybody. I was an equal opportunity provider, happy to provide for free when a local shelter was low on formula and needed to supplement. Or to my premium skin-to-skin clients at top dollar. And all those in between. And then there were those who needed to buy frozen, usually because they were traveling and wouldn't be able to take fresh milk on the road for extended periods of time.

And some of my clients were damn addicts. The thought made me smile. If they had to go a day without milk, they were convinced their health would fail or all their gains would be lost. Silly but good for business.

After pumping as much as I could, I went for my morning run. I was three miles into it and on an uphill stretch when my phone rang. It was my business line, so I slowed down to a jog and answered the call. "Chad's Power Milk. How can I help you?"

The line was quiet, but it sounded like there was someone there. I pulled the phone away from my ear to make sure we had a good connection. "Hello, this is Chad. Can I help you?"

And then the call disconnected. Probably a wrong number.

I slipped my phone back into the pocket built into my shorts and headed up the hill. With just a few blocks left until I was home, my phone rang again from the same number.

Occasionally, a customer would call who was a little nervous about identifying themselves. It didn't happen often, but there had been a few times in the past. My mind immediately went to the boy from the club. *Could it be him?*

"Hello, this is Chad. What's your name?"

There was a short bout of silence before I heard a soft voice say, "Ricky."

"Thanks for calling, Ricky." I placed my hand on my hip and took a deep breath so I wasn't panting. "Did we meet the other night?"

The line was quiet, but I could almost imagine him shaking his head.

"You might have felt too shy to meet me, so you got out of line?"

"Maybe."

Yes, it was him. "All right, sweetheart. I'm happy to answer any questions that you have, but it would be easier for us to do this in person so I can see your responses a little bit better than having to hear them."

"Okay."

I thought about our options and then looked at my watch. I had to drop off a quart at the medspa downtown. They used it for some sort of facial they probably charged a thousand dollars for, so I took a chance and put it out there. "I'm gonna be at the Java Hut on California Avenue at ten-thirty this morning. Would you like to meet me there so we can talk?"

"Okay." Again, it was barely a whisper, and I wasn't sure he'd actually show up, but that was the best I could do.

"All right, Ricky. I'll grab a table and you come find me when you're ready."

It was almost nine, so I had plenty of time to shower, pump, and stake out a table at the Java Hut. I wanted to be ready and in a semi-private spot if he did show up. And if he didn't, I had some emails I could respond to while I waited.

I wasn't due at the spa until eleven-thirty, so I had plenty of time to kill, and I couldn't imagine doing anything better than waiting for a sweet boy to find the courage to speak with me.

After dropping my stuff at a table facing the front door, I bought two bottles of water and ordered a cup of herbal tea. I wanted to make it easy for Ricky to find me when he came in, but still provide enough space for him to decide if and when he was ready to join me.

And even though I really wanted a cup of coffee, heavy on the black, I had to keep my caffeine levels in check while I was feeding the babies. Small amounts of caffeine was fine for healthy babies, but with preemies, I didn't want to take any chances.

Tea seemed to help my production level anyway, so it was a win-win all the way around.

At exactly ten twenty-nine, the door opened, and Ricky walked in.

I tried to keep my eyes down, not putting pressure on him to approach me, but when he stood by the door for several seconds, I couldn't resist. I glanced up and smiled and then waved him over. "Come on in, Ricky. Have a seat."

He inhaled deeply and slowly walked toward me. After standing by the chair for a moment, he carefully dropped into the seat across from me. "Hi."

Fuck, he was cute. I mean, he was adorable in his little sailor jammies at the club, but dressed up for work in a polo and chinos was almost cuter. "It's really nice to meet you, Ricky. I'm glad you came."

He nodded and rolled his lip between his teeth, debating whether to speak.

I could tell he wasn't comfortable, so I did my best to put him at ease. I got you a water, but if you'd like something to drink or maybe a pastry, I can go get that for you. Do you drink coffee?

He shook his head and then cleared his throat. "Usually just hot cocoa."

It was a risk, but I took the opportunity to lighten the tension. "A milk man. I can appreciate that." I winked and stood up from the table. "One hot cocoa coming up."

At the counter, I ordered his cocoa with whipped cream, taking my time getting back so he had a moment to gather himself. Poor boy looked like he was gonna burst into tears or run from the building. Possibly both.

Time to turn on the charm, Chad. "I'm probably not supposed to say this, but I was a little disappointed when you got out of line."

His jaw dropped open, and he looked surprised. "I'm sorry. It wasn't your fault. I was just…shy."

"You don't have to apologize, sweetheart. Lots of people are shy. I just thought you looked so cute in your sailor jammies, and I wanted to meet you."

"You did?" he whispered. "Why?"

Why, indeed. "Well, of all the boys and girls there, you're the one who caught my eye." I figured honesty was the best policy with this kid, and either it would work…or it wouldn't. "I hope I'm not being too forward."

"You're not, if you're telling the truth."

That wasn't the response I expected. "Do you think I'm not telling the truth?"

He shrugged and glanced up, meeting my gaze for a moment before looking away again. "It's hard to believe. There were a lot of people there, and…I'm not special."

Oh, yes, sweetheart. You definitely are. I wanted so bad to reach across the table and brush my finger across his cheek or hold his hand against my lips. But we definitely weren't ready for contact. "You seem pretty special to me." I took a deep breath and leaned back in my chair, putting a little bit more space between us so he wouldn't feel intimidated. "So, do you have any questions I can answer? Maybe you'd like to set up a private session?"

His whole face got red as he reached for his mug and took a sip. "Yeah, maybe." He took a sip as soon as the words were out as if the distraction might make me forget.

Oh, I could never forget you. "Okay, we can definitely do that. I have openings for house calls later this week, and of course, I also sell fresh and frozen milk if you'd be more comfortable with that."

He looked up at me with a completely different expression on his face. "Like, in a cup?"

I chuckled and nodded. "Yeah, you can put it in a cup. I'll provide it in a bag, but some people will drink it in a smoothie or in their coffee…or from a bottle. Whatever you'd like."

His jaw hung open for a moment as he just looked at me, evaluating what I'd just said. "What about the other way? Like…on the couch."

Yes, now we were getting somewhere. "The freshest of the fresh." I placed my hand over my heart and gave a little tap. "Direct from the source would be my preference too, if you'd like to try that."

He nodded just enough for me to notice and then looked away. "Um, where? Like, do I go to you or do you come to me?"

"I travel throughout the greater Seattle area. Are you local?"

"Yeah, I have a house on Forest Street. Is that okay?"

I cocked my head and pulled up the map app on my phone. "Oh, that's only a few miles from my place. I'm on the other side of the park on Bradford. Would you like to meet at your place? Do you live alone?"

He sighed and gave me a sad smile. "Yeah. Very alone."

4

RICKY

I wasn't sure he would recognize me when I walked into the café wearing my work clothes. I looked nothing like I did at the club, but Chad's eyes instantly locked on to me, and I knew he knew.

It took all the courage I could muster just to approach the table and sit down, but I did it. Even though I was terrified that I was making a huge mistake.

But Chad seemed to know exactly what to say to put me at ease. When he brought up the topic of a private session, I was so grateful I didn't have to say the words out loud. It was hard enough to look him in the eye because my gaze was constantly drifting to his chest where I really wanted to get a closer look.

As excited as I was for my session, I needed to keep reminding myself that I was just a customer.

He was coming to see me because I was paying him to—not because he liked me. And that was okay.

I definitely wouldn't expect a gorgeous Daddy-type like Chad to be interested in a scrawny number nerd like myself. I just hoped I didn't become addicted. His private rate wasn't cheap, and if it was even a fraction as good as I was imagining it would be, I might have to take out a second mortgage on my house.

"All right, Ricky. Snap out of it. Time to focus." I opened up my laptop and ignored the four tabs of social media pages I had open up to low-key stalk Chad. Okay, it was high-key stalking. Very high-key.

As in, I accidentally liked every photo in his feed, and I left at least half a dozen heart reactions to his selfies. The man posted a lot of selfies. And why shouldn't he? He was everything a man should be…and even had something special that a guy like me never even dreamed possible.

"Focus, Ricky." Right! Back to ignoring Chad's pictures as I expanded the spreadsheet to full screen.

I'd already figured out that the cash deposits went down five out of seven days a week over the past several months, and one of two employees was always working on those dates. Which made it easy to narrow down the embezzler for my medspa client.

But what I wasn't sure of was how much was taken. That required a much deeper dive into all the services performed each day based on an entirely different database. But that was where I shone.

And in a strange turn of events, or maybe it was kismet, the client Chad was making a delivery to was my medspa client. He mentioned being at the coffee shop because he had a delivery down the street. Which got me wondering how many other clients I might've had that could benefit from the delivery side of his service.

Not that I had any reason to want him out of the "personal house call" business. Maybe I could win the lotto and buy him exclusively. And then, I would be the only one who could ever taste his skin.

"Focus already, dammit." I opened up the service logs for the first location and began the arduous task of matching receipts to employees to services.

Never a dull moment in the world of forensic accounting. And I didn't mean that ironically.

I actually thrived on that stuff.

Chad told me to dress comfortably for our session.

One outfit came to mind when I thought about being truly comfortable, but I wasn't sure it was appropriate. Then again, he said he liked it. So, after debating with myself for almost an hour, I put on my sailor pajamas and slipped a pair of sweats and a hoodie over it.

They were ready to reveal if the moment was right, but hidden if it didn't feel appropriate.

I didn't wanna make things awkward between us, especially if there was even the slightest chance of making this an ongoing arrangement. If I could pick up a side hustle, maybe delivering meals or groceries on the weekends, I could totally pay for one or two sessions with him every week.

But I was getting ahead of myself. I hadn't even had one session yet. What if I didn't like it? Maybe it would be weird and awkward and I would never want to do it again.

Before I could get too far into my head, the doorbell rang.

It was him. We were really gonna do this.

I took a deep breath and opened the front door, pulling out as much courage as I possibly could to get through the next hour. When I saw how good he looked, I just stood there and stared.

"Hi, Ricky." He took a step back and slipped his hands in his pockets. "Is this still a good time?"

"Yeah. Come in." I hesitated for another second before stepping out of the way so he could follow me inside.

Chad closed the door behind me and turned the deadbolt.

A flash of anxiety went through me because he locked the door, but then I realized the door needed to be locked. I would never be able to relax if I knew somebody might walk in on us. Not that anyone would ever walk into my house, but I still appreciated the gesture. "Thank you."

He took a few steps into the entryway and then kicked off his shoes, looking at me and waiting for directions.

From me? I was supposed to tell him what to do next? "Um, how do we do this?"

Chad took one look at the way I was trembling and spread open his arms. "If you're comfortable with it, I'd like to start with a hug. You look like you could use it."

I swallowed hard and nodded, stepping right up into his embrace. His arms instinctively closed around me, and mine wrapped around him too. Inhaling deeply against his shoulder brought me a sense of security I needed. I was feeling better already. "Thanks," I whispered.

"Would you like to have a seat on your sofa?"

I nodded and pointed toward the living room.

Chad reached for my hand, and when I placed mine on top of his, he slowly walked me over to the couch. "Do you have a preference to be on one side or the other?"

I shook my head, feeling more comfortable without having to use words.

"How about I sit down and you can maybe rest your head on my lap while we talk for a little while. Is that okay?"

My eyes were locked on his again as I nodded and lowered my hand in front of my crotch to hide the fact that I was beginning to get hard.

If Chad noticed my hand, he didn't acknowledge it. He just sat down in the corner of the couch and put one of the throw pillows over his lap. "If you'd like, I can tell you a story."

I bit my lower lip and nodded eagerly as I sat down beside him, facing the back of the couch before I slowly lowered my head onto the pillow over his lap.

Chad's fingers brushed through the top of my hair, combing it to the side so it was out of my face as I looked up at him.

My eyes jumped between looking at his chest and his face, but mostly I kept sneaking glances at his chest, knowing what was hidden beneath his button-down shirt.

He even smelled really good as I scooted a tiny bit closer to him.

"Once upon a time, there was a little boy who set off in a sailboat to find pirates…"

5

CHAD

It took a few minutes for the tension throughout Ricky's body to relax so he could really melt into the couch. He was stiff in my lap as his eyes danced between my mouth and my chest.

But by the time I got to the part about the boy jumping into the water to swim with some dolphins, Ricky had inched close enough that his nose was up against my shirt.

As casually as I could, I unbuttoned my top button while I kept talking, carefully watching him to make sure he wasn't startled.

Ricky licked his lips as he watched my fingers slowly move to the next button. By the time my shirt was fully separated, he seemed ready. "Ricky, are you ready to give this a try?"

He nodded and looked up at me, meeting my gaze. "How?"

"If it's okay with you, I'll lift you up so you're in position, and when you're ready, just put your mouth on me and try to suck. It usually takes a few tries to get a good seal, but you'll figure it out." I couldn't resist brushing the side of his cheek with my finger and trailing it around his ear.

His eyes drifted shut for a moment at the contact before opening his eyes again. "Yes, please."

I could see the neckline of his pajamas underneath his hoodie, but if he was comfortable in what he was wearing, I wasn't gonna interrupt this moment for a wardrobe change.

Slipping my arm underneath his back, I gently lifted him up so he was in line with my chest. And, as usually happened, instincts took over and he knew exactly where to place his mouth.

Ricky's soft lips were tentative at first, and then I felt his tongue swipe across my tip and I almost moaned myself.

A BORN PROVIDER

This was a job.

I was being paid.

Nothing more was gonna happen, but…damn, I was already hard.

I'd never appreciated a pillow in my lap as much as I did when the first wave of milk filled his mouth.

Also as expected, Ricky's eyes opened in surprise, and he looked up at me.

I gave him a gentle smile and rubbed along his jawline. "You got it, sweetheart. Go ahead and take as much as you need. And if you want to hop onto the other side too, there's plenty for you."

A small whimper vibrated over my skin as he closed his eyes and began a steady rhythm of sucking and licking my nipple. Within just a few minutes, his other hand wandered up and began to twist and tease my other nipple, something I was ridiculously sensitive to.

God, that felt good.

I didn't usually let customers do it, but I wasn't about to stop him. The sweet boy in my arms could do just about anything he wanted.

And that was gonna be my problem.

As milk drunk as Ricky was getting, I was equally lust drunk from staring at him.

He was the absolute perfect mix of innocence and sweetness that I adored in a boy. I regretted not asking him to take off his outer layer so I could see him in his jammies, but maybe another time.

Would there be another time? Fuck, I hoped so.

When his fingers' ministrations stimulated a steady flow of milk down my right side, Ricky's eyes popped open and he looked at me.

"It's okay, sweetheart. If you want to switch over, you can. Or you can just keep doing what you're doing." I rubbed the swell of his hip and rested my hand at his waist. "You're doing just fine."

He gently pulled off my left nipple and then scooted down so he was aligned on my other side.

We had to adjust the pillow, and he curled around me a little more thoroughly to find a comfortable position, but once he was there, his eyes rolled back and he drifted off again to that happy space that he seemed to get lost in.

The story I'd been telling him was long forgotten, and I wasn't sure if talking would break the spell he was under or coax him to regress even further. I decided to go with a tactic that I was pretty sure would work.

Praise.

"You're such a good boy, Ricky. Drinking all your milk so you have a full tummy."

He sighed and sucked a little faster. His hand slid into his pants, but his eyes never opened. Maybe he wasn't aware of what he was doing, but I sure as fuck was…

And so was my dick.

"That's right, sweetheart. Take what you need. Take Daddy's milk and feel good."

His hand started to move faster inside his pants.

Since I knew he was wearing those pajamas, I had to assume he was rubbing himself through the fabric. I wanted so badly for this to be a personal call, so I could reach inside and help him out.

But that wasn't why I was here.

Instead, I did everything I could to avoid thinking about what he was doing.

What he was about to do.

I glanced around the room and saw a neat pile of magazines on top of a bookshelf on the opposite side of the room. On the shelves, row after row of paperbacks were arranged by height, but I couldn't tell what genre they were from where I was sitting. And in the far corner of the love seat to my right, a mint-green piece of silicone stuck out from the cushion, and I recognized it instantly.

It was the same kind of pacifier we used in the hospital.

Clearly, Ricky's oral fixation ran deep. *Fuck, could he be any more perfect?*

The suction on my nipple increased, and I glanced down to see his whole body arch up off the couch as he came in his pajamas.

I should have ignored it.

I usually ignored this kind of thing if it happened with a client, always giving them space and privacy to enjoy their session however they chose. But I was as mesmerized as he was until his mouth popped off me. I instantly looked at his eyes and saw the tears building up before they poured down his face. "I'm so sorry. I'm so sorry."

"Hey, it's okay, sweetheart." I wrapped both arms around his back and pulled him up higher, resting his head against my shoulder as I gently rocked us both. "You did nothing wrong. I'm very happy that you enjoyed your session, and I hope we can do this again."

He sobbed a few times before his thumb slipped into his mouth and he looked up at me. "Again?" he said around his thumb.

"If you'd like to. There's no pressure, but I enjoyed my time here with you." Against my better judgment, I leaned forward and placed a kiss on his forehead. "I think you're someone very special, Ricky."

He took a shuddering breath and pulled his thumb out so he could wrap his arm around my neck and get even closer to me. "I think you're special too, Chad."

It was obvious Ricky wasn't ready to be alone, so I pulled the blanket off the back of the couch and tucked it around him so he was bundled up in my arms. "I'll stay here as long as you need me."

"You're a good Daddy." His thumb went into his mouth, and he nodded.

I smiled at that and rubbed the side of my thumb up and down his neck. "It's easy when I'm with such a good boy."

Ricky turned into me for a second as his ears pinked up. "I wish you were my Daddy."

I swallowed hard, not allowing myself to get sucked into the moment. It wasn't uncommon for a Little to regress to the point of saying things they didn't mean. Not really. But it was my job to keep things professional, even though that was harder and harder by the second. Literally. "I work a lot, so I probably wouldn't be a great Daddy. Always pumping and making deliveries. It's not all fun and games being a milk factory."

Ricky smiled and let his thumb slip from his mouth. "Do you have a lot of little boys like me?"

That was a loaded question. "I have a few clients who are sweet little boys like you." I tickled his side and made him giggle. "But mostly, I work with grownups who have strict dietary requirements. My training is as a clinical dietician, but I've just naturally evolved into a milkman over the years because it's so lucrative."

"That means 'spensive."

Okay, so he was still regressed but slowing coming out of it. "Yep, it can be expensive."

"What does the medspa need milk for?"

"They use it to make some special creams and masks. Facials and skin treatments, I think. I take a few quarts of frozen milk to a few facilities each week." It was a decent contract.

Ricky nodded. "I might know of a few other companies who would be interested in your services."

"Yeah?" I was surprised he was back in work mode so easily. "Feel free to pass on my number. I don't take a lot of in-person clients, but I can make room for one or two more."

The smile on Ricky's face morphed into a frown and he sat up, putting some distance between us. "Thank you for coming tonight. I really enjoyed it."

"Me too." I scooted forward as I buttoned up my shirt. "Is everything alright, Ricky."

He just nodded and stared straight ahead, back to nonverbal cues.

"Ricky." I took his hand in mine and clasped it close to

my mouth. "If I said something to upset you, I'm sorry. I didn't mean to."

He sighed heavily and his chin dropped to his chest. "I'm just jealous."

"Jealous?" I ignored the alarm bells ringing in my head and let my instincts take over. I slipped one arm under his thighs and lifted him back onto my lap, this time without the pillow separating us. "Of what, baby boy?"

His forehead pressed against the crook of my neck, and he licked across my skin, making a shiver run down my spine and directly into my cock. "Of every person who gets to drink your Daddy milk."

Fuck me. I had no response to that, so I just held him tighter against me, hoping I didn't do anything to screw this up.

6

CHAD

I barely made it home before I had to pump. In general, I produced a lot, but I rarely leaked like this. Something was up. I was sure that Ricky had sucked me dry, at least for a few hours. But apparently, he spurred some kind of super flood that kept me attached to the damn pump all night long.

Not only that, I was horny as fuck.

I couldn't remember the last time I needed to get off like this. Not just a perfunctory thing to do because I was hard in the morning. It was like something inside me needed to be unleashed.

He'd unleashed something in me.

And it wasn't just physical attraction. I felt different with him.

He was different. When he looked at me, he saw more than just the milk I could provide. He listened to every word I said, as if each one was important. And every smile I flashed in his direction was rewarded with one of equal brilliance.

Not to mention how sweet he was. He offered so much tenderness that it made me want to melt at his perfect mix of innocence and delight.

I'd never felt like this before, especially about a client. But I already knew he was more than just a client. I just wasn't sure if he knew it yet.

It might be a slow process with him. I couldn't push. I needed to let him set the pace, even though he also wanted a Daddy to guide him. Which made this a delicate balance of taking charge and standing back that I'd have to carefully navigate.

After pumping, I went straight to the shower and got cleaned up. I had a long day between two hospital visits, client prep and deliveries, and maybe the most important meeting of my life.

The hot water felt good as it pounded against my back. I pressed my forehead on the tile wall and just let my muscles loosen up. Every time I closed my eyes, I thought about Ricky on my chest, sucking like he'd been stranded in the desert for days and only I could quench his thirst.

And when his hand slipped into his pants and I knew he was rubbing his cock because of me...

Fuck.

I reached for mine and began stroking, moving in rhythm with the Ricky in my mind, moaning and sucking and looking up at me with that innocence that made me want to pull him into my arms and protect him from the world.

That's right, baby. Come for Daddy.

The memory of Ricky arching off the couch as he came pushed me over the edge, and I shot hot come onto the shower wall, letting it mix with the water circling the drain. After riding out the orgasm, I turned around and rinsed it from my body.

I definitely needed to see him again.

Soon. But for now, I'd do my best to give him some space. I couldn't guarantee how long that would last, but if I came on too strong, I might scare him away. And that was the last thing I wanted.

Hell, if I thought it would be good for him, I might not have ever left him alone. But at least for tonight, we both got a little bit of what we needed.

I just hoped there was room for a lot more in our future… Together.

For the next few days, I was strong.

I did my work and pumped like an oil rig, but I was able to give Ricky some space. Until I couldn't. By Wednesday, I was at my tipping point.

Apparently, he was too, because just as I was just leaving the hospital, I got a text that made my heart speed up. ***Can I buy another session?***

I had to take a moment to carefully word my response. I needed to make sure he knew that I was eager for another session with him, but I didn't want him to pay for it. I wanted it to be personal… And I didn't know how to say that without being creepy. ***Yes, I'd love to see you again. What day are you free?***

His response was immediate. *Maybe Friday. I get off work at five, so anytime after.*

I pulled up my calendar app to check my schedule. On Friday, I had an appointment at four with my trainer, and then I had to make a few deliveries with clients, but then I'd be free until Saturday morning when I was due at the hospital. *If it's not too late, I can be there at 7 o'clock on Friday. I'm happy to bring dinner as well.*

Dinner sounds nice... How much extra does that cost?

I took a deep breath and thumbed out the words I hoped he'd accept as they were intended. *No charge for dinner. It's my treat. And if you're comfortable with it, I'd like to see you on Friday as a date instead of a client. So no charge for any of it. What do you think?* After I sent the text, I immediately followed up with an out, just in case he needed one. *If you'd like to keep it professional, that's okay too. Just respond back with either "date" or "professional" and we'll move forward accordingly.*

The response dots came up and disappeared four times over the next minute before he finally pushed send. *Date, please.*

I'm looking forward to it. Do you have any suggestions for dinner or should I pick something?

Pick anything, but I like noodles.

I chuckled as I responded back. ***I love noodles too, and I know just the place to get them.***

With a new spring in my step, I headed home to pick up everything I needed for my evening deliveries. Part of me was disappointed that Ricky wasn't available to see me immediately, but at least I knew he was as anxious as I was for another visit.

If nothing else, at least we'd get to find out if there was more chemistry to our relationship than nursing. I was almost positive there was, but we needed a nonprofessional visit to be sure.

And once we knew, I was willing to go as slow as he needed.

I was very sure he'd be worth it.

7

RICKY

At eight-thirty, I was already curled up in bed with a book when I got a text.

Sometimes work messages came in late but usually not that late. That made me worried something was wrong, so I rolled over and pulled my phone off the charger.

It was a text from Chad.

My heart started racing as I opened it up. And when I saw the meme with a baby kitten that said *Have a purr-fectly good night*, I wanted to respond with a request for him to come right over and put me to bed.

But I couldn't do that.

I had to be a patient boy, even though it was killing me. But if I waited until Friday afternoon, I'd have the whole weekend to think about Chad. Think about and reminisce how wonderful my time with him was, because I knew it would be. And I wanted to have a lot of time to think about it before work.

If I had scheduled our date for tonight, I wouldn't have been able to focus on work tomorrow or Friday, and that would just get me into trouble. And I hated getting into trouble.

So, I'd work until Friday and then be able to completely focus on Daddy Chad. I just had to remember not to call him that to his face until he said it was okay. And I really hoped he'd say it was okay on Friday. More than anything, I wanted to call him Daddy on our date.

I did a quick search for a funny accounting meme and finally found one with a sloth hanging on a branch and it said, "I'd say good night too, but I don't think you'd depreciate it." I wasn't sure he'd understand it, but I sent it anyway, hoping he wouldn't think I was too stuffy.

He immediately responded back with a laughing emoji and a heart.

A heart.

He sent me a heart. It wasn't a declaration and probably didn't mean anything, but I let myself pretend it did. I pretended it meant he thought I was a special boy who deserved a good Daddy like him.

And when I slipped my pacifier back into my mouth, I kept pretending…but this time, it was that I was sucking on Chad instead.

For the next two days, I did my best to focus on my work and not obsess over Friday evening. But it was really hard.

I just couldn't stop thinking about how his muscles felt under my fingertips when I touched Chad's chest and how soft his nipple was when I pulled it into my mouth and sucked his milk right out of him.

Every time I relived my session, I would get hard and have to run into the bathroom to take care of it.

And it didn't help that he kept sending me sweet and silly messages. Every morning, there would be a cute good morning meme waiting for me on my phone. And throughout the day, he checked in on me.

He even asked if I had been drinking enough water when I mentioned getting a headache yesterday afternoon.

Chad was always taking care of me, and I was starting to get more jealous about all the other people he was taking care of.

But I had to share… Especially since he wasn't actually mine to be possessive of.

And even if he ever did agree to be my Daddy, I would still have to share him. He had a successful business, and I would never stand in the way of him making a living from his milk.

But if he ever decided to only sell pumped milk to other people, that would be okay with me.

Ugh, what was I thinking? He's not my Daddy.

I had to keep reminding myself of that. Why was it so hard for me to wrap my brain around the fact that one first date did not mean a lifetime commitment.

Although, it didn't mean there wouldn't be one, so…a boy could dream.

At lunchtime on Friday, I went to the kink store attached to Lashes and Lace and bought myself some new pajamas. This set was also cuffed at the ankles, but the zipper started at the front and the back. I could unzip it from my neck down and wrap it all the way between my legs and around over my bottom… Or I could leave the front zipped up and only unzip the backside.

It was made for sexy times, and I really wanted to have some sexy times with Chad.

But also, I didn't wanna make a mess like I did last time. If nothing else happened, at least I could take my dick out and come on my blankie if things got to that point…if Chad was okay with that. Should I ask if he was okay with that? He didn't say anything about it last time, but he had to know what I did.

As soon as I was finished with my work for the day, I took an extra good shower to make sure every part of me was fresh and clean, and then I slipped on my new pajamas. And then a worry filled my mind.

What if he wants to go out?

I was pretty sure I knew the answer to that, but I wanted to make sure, so I sent him a quick text. **Will we be staying in tonight?** As soon as I hit send, I slipped my phone into my pocket and pulled out the vacuum.

When I was done vacuuming, I checked his response. *That's my plan, unless you'd like to go out.*

Nope. Just deciding what to wear. I thought about it for a second and then shot off another text just to put it out there. *I bought a new pair of jammies.*

I can't wait to see them.

He wanted to see them. A little flutter happened in my tummy as I pictured opening my door in my PJs. What would he be wearing? That gave me an idea, so I sent him another text. *I'd like for you to be as comfortable as possible, so you can wear pajamas too, if you'd like.*

Chad sent back a smiling emoji with heart eyes. *I sleep in the buff, but I can wear gym clothes, if that's OK.*

That's very OK. I wanted us to have easy access…so maybe we could also fit in a workout of sorts. *See you soon.*

I can't wait.

I couldn't wait either. I wanted to sit on the couch and stare at the door until the doorbell rang.

Instead, I filled a big glass with water and drank that, knowing it would help with that tiny headache that was starting to throb right behind my eyes. I really needed to stay hydrated throughout the day.

If only there were someone who could help with that...

8

CHAD

I planned on wearing jeans again, but after Ricky's suggestion to come in my pajamas, I decided to switch it up. I put on a pair of slim joggers and a tight-fitting performance shirt then headed out the door.

I didn't usually walk around like that, because when I wore that outfit at the gym, I always got a lot of attention. From just about everyone. So, I knew Ricky would likely appreciate how I looked.

There was a group of food trucks that showed up downtown every Friday night, so I swung by there and went to my favorite mac-and-cheese truck. They had a five-flavor flight that was absolutely amazing, and I had a feeling Ricky would like it too.

I also got buttered breadsticks, but without the garlic. If things got a little bit heated tonight, I didn't wanna have garlic breath.

And I wanted things to get heated.

I'd been careful not to be too flirty in my texts to Ricky, but on several occasions, I had to stop myself from asking him to send me a photo. I didn't want him to think I forgot what he looked like—I could never forget—but almost worse than that, I didn't want him to think about what I would be doing while I stared at his picture.

It seemed crazy to me, but I'd forgotten what it was like to have a heightened libido.

For so long, sex had just been a quick release or an afterthought when I was hanging out with someone I enjoyed being around. Like a goodbye kiss on a decent but not amazing date. Just a night cap that I could take or leave…but felt like a nice gesture.

Not at all how I imagined being with Ricky would be. Since meeting him, sex was all I could think about. I wanted to touch him… And I wanted him to touch me. Not just on my chest but everywhere.

Fuck, I was starting to get hard again. And if I wasn't careful, I'd start leaking too.

I put off my second session with the babies as late as possible so I could get through at least a few hours without pumping, but whatever was happening to my body was making me hyperproduce.

It was annoying as fuck…and constant.

I sure hoped Ricky was thirsty because he was gonna get a flood.

When I arrived at his place, I parked in front at the curb. By the time I started walking up to his porch, Ricky had the door open and was standing there in his new pajamas. They had teddy bears all over and were adorable. But what was even more interesting to me was the zipper. It started at his neck and went all the way down his front before it disappeared under his crotch.

I wondered how far up it went in the back. *Nope. Not the time to think about that.*

I held up the bag of mac & cheese in one hand and a small box of eclairs in the other that I picked up at a pastry truck. "I hope you're hungry."

Ricky bit his lip and nodded. "Starving." He stepped back as soon as I approached his doorway and ushered me in with a wave of his arm. "Come in and make yourself comfortable."

"Thank you." I slipped out of my sneakers then went straight to his kitchen and placed everything on the table before turning to him with spread arms. "Do I get a hug?"

He didn't say anything as he rushed to me, wrapping his arms around my middle and pressing his nose into the crook of my neck. "You smell so…warm."

I laughed at that. "Is that a nice way of saying I'm sweaty?"

"No. Not that kind of warm." He inhaled again, his nose brushing against my skin. "More comfy than warm, I guess. Like, fresh out of the shower warm." He looked up at me and grinned. "Is that better?"

"Yeah, it actually is." I leaned forward and kissed his cheek. "You look adorable, by the way. I love the new jams."

He stepped back and spread his arms out to show off the full effect. "Thank you."

I reached for the pull of the zipper that was hanging right under his neck and gave it a little tap. "And this is an interesting zipper."

His face went red as he sucked in a deep breath. "It goes all the way around."

"Oh yeah? Can I see?"

He swallowed hard as he nodded and then slowly turned in a circle.

Shit, it went right up his ass. Definitely made for easy access. "I love it. I've never seen one like that before."

"I got it today." His back was to me as he headed to the kitchen. "At Lashes and Lace."

Interesting. I walked past their store when I was there, but I assumed it was more of a convenience store for condoms and Gatorade. I didn't realize they sold clothes. "Well, you look very cute and comfy."

Ricky grabbed some plates from his cabinet and placed them on the table before looking at me. "I am." He smiled shyly then opened a drawer and pulled out utensils. "Will we need knives?"

"Probably not. I brought five flavors of mac and cheese

and bread. But the bread is already baked in a lot of butter, so I don't know if you'll need to add extra."

He put the two knives he was holding back in the drawer and closed it with his hip. "No knives. I don't want extra." He cleared his throat as he turned toward the refrigerator. "I need to make sure I save room."

I definitely wanted him to save room too. "That's a smart decision."

"So…what would you like to drink? I have filtered water, lemonade, beer that might be flat from Christmas time, and…lemon lime soda."

"Lemonade sounds good." I began unbagging the containers and set them up in the center of his table.

He pulled out a pitcher of lemonade and poured two glasses. One was a full pint glass that he placed on one side of the table, closer to me, and the other was a small juice cup that was about half full.

"Not very thirsty?" I grinned, anticipating his response.

This boy didn't disappoint. He shrugged one shoulder and glanced up at me with a smirk. "Saving room."

Good boy.

As soon as I opened the first container, Ricky moaned and dropped down into a chair, just watching me in awe. "That smells so good…and looks even more delicious."

"I haven't tried all these, but every one that I have tried in the past is delicious." I gave him a spoonful from each container and a piece of bread before serving myself the same and sitting down. "So, how was your day?"

He sighed as he picked up his fork. "Busy. Long. Frustrating. Full of anticipation." Ricky scooped a bite of lobster mac & cheese into his mouth, and his eyes rolled back as he moaned. "But it was all worth it for this moment."

9

RICKY

I did my best to take a bite of every flavor, but it was so rich and delicious that I was already getting full after my fourth bite. And then there were the rolls. It would have been rude not to eat at least a few bites of bread, but I just didn't think I could do it.

But I tried.

And a little groan snuck out of my throat.

"You okay, sweetheart?" Chad slid his socked foot across the tile floor and hooked it behind my ankle.

I peeked up at him. "I'm getting full, but it's all so good. I want to try everything."

He cocked his head and his eyebrows furrowed. "Not if it's gonna give you a tummy ache." He put his fork down and wiped his mouth with a napkin. "Why don't we save the rest of this for later. Maybe a snack or lunch tomorrow?"

"Oh." I suddenly felt better. That was a much smarter plan than eating myself nauseous and not being able to have any milk later. "Okay. And thank you."

"Of course." He stood up and started covering up the containers.

"I can do that."

"Not at all. Just rest for a few minutes while I get these in the fridge, and then we can watch a movie." He piled three containers on top of each other and then looked back at me. "If you're still up for that. If not, I can take a raincheck."

"No." I jumped to my feet and started helping him clean up. "Please don't leave. I feel fine. I just need a break before…" I swallowed and felt my neck warming. "Well, you know."

"If you're sure." He stacked the leftovers neatly in the fridge and then turned around with a can of lemon lime soda. "This might help settle your stomach."

It had been a long time since someone wanted to take

care of me without me asking for help. "Thank you, Da— I mean, thanks."

His gaze held me in place for a few seconds before he slipped his arm behind my back and guided me to the sofa. "Would you like to be in here or in bed for movie time?"

Oh, that was an interesting question. "Is it okay if we watch in my bed?"

"Of course." He held me a little closer to his side. "Lead the way."

We went into my bedroom, and I stood in the middle of the room, halfway between the bed and the bathroom. I glanced at both, not sure which way to go.

Chad slid his hand up to the back of my neck and clasped it like he owned me. "Do you need to go potty before the movie?"

I nodded and looked up at him.

"Do you want any help?" He reached for the top of the zipper and gave it a gentle tug, just enough to move it a few inches.

I wanted to say yes. So badly. But I was too embarrassed. What if I did it wrong? So I dropped my shoulders and shook my head. "I'll be okay."

"That's not what I asked, sweetheart." He pulled his hand around and cupped my cheek. "I asked if you want any help."

"Yes, but…" I felt silly saying it out loud, but I didn't know exactly what he meant. "I'm not sure what that means."

He nodded and reached for my hand, tugging me toward the bathroom. Without a word, he positioned me so I was standing in front of the toilet. "Stand or sit?"

"Stand."

Chad's chest pressed to my back, and he reached around me, slowly lowering my zipper with his fingers tucked inside to make sure nothing got caught. After he passed over my dick, he placed one hand on my chest to steady me. With his other hand, he closed his fingers around my wrist and brought my hand to where it needed to be. "Go ahead, sweetheart."

I reached for myself and peed with his arms securely holding me. When I was done, he helped me zip up and wash my hands before we headed back to the bed.

Chad pulled back the covers on the side closest to the door and then smoothed down the sheet. "Do you need anything else before getting in?"

"No, thank you." I crawled in and pulled my small blankie out from under my pillow and grabbed my big silicone pacifier. Then I handed the remote to Chad.

"Am I in charge of this?" He took the remote and got comfortable beside me on the bed, plumping up the pillows against the headboard before leaning back.

I nodded and leaned against his side as I put the pacifier in my mouth and curled my first around my blankie. Everything was perfect. I was beside the best Daddy I'd ever met, and he knew exactly how to take care of me.

I had everything I needed…in my bed.

Da— Um, Chad put on a funny movie about a bunch of guys who set up a summer camp for grownups, and they got into a bunch of silly situations. I laughed a lot, but mostly, I cuddled up with the sexy Daddy in my bed.

By the time the movie was at the halfway point, my eyelids were getting heavy. I had such big plans for our night, but then I was too sleepy to do all the fun stuff. I spit out the pacifier and sighed loudly.

"Everything okay?" Chad paused the movie and lifted my chin so he could look into my eyes.

I shrugged and then brushed my face against Chad's chest. He looked so good in that tight shirt and... "You're leaking."

"Oh." He pulled the shirt off his skin and seemed to notice the wet spots for the first time. "Sorry. That's been happening a lot more often these days."

I bit my lip and slipped my fingertips to the bottom edge of his shirt. "Can I help?"

10

CHAD

So much for taking things slow.

I was already in his fucking bed and had handled his dick. There wasn't much room for a slow reveal after this…and he was as into it as I was.

"That would be great. Thank you." I turned slightly toward him and smiled. "Is there anything you'd like me to do before we get started?"

"Could you turn off the big lights so it's cozy in here?"

"Of course." I scooted off the bed and turned off the overhead light. As soon as it was dark, three color-coordinated LED lights came on in different corners of the room, providing enough illumination to get around but not enough to be annoying when sleeping. "Anything else while I'm up?"

Ricky pursed his lips like he was trying to keep himself from speaking and then gripped his blanket against his chest with both hands. "Can you stay tonight?"

"Like, until you fall asleep?"

He shrugged and twisted his blanket some more. "Or 'til morning." His gaze shot up and connected with mine again. "So I can help you in the morning too. That's when it's worse, right? That's what I read, anyway."

I grinned and headed back to his bed, pulling my shirt over my head on my way but keeping it with me as a towel in case one side started to leak. I stepped out of my joggers too. I would be way too hot to sleep in them. "Doing some research, huh?"

His eyes were wide as he looked at me in just my black boxer briefs and then cleared his throat to refocus. "Yeah, well, I want to do a good job." His voice was so low I barely heard him. "So…you know."

I pulled back the covers on the other side of his bed

and slipped in, making myself comfortable. "I know...what?"

He just shrugged and looked away, like he didn't want to give voice to whatever he was thinking.

Letting it go for now, I propped myself up on my elbow and faced him. "How will you be most comfortable to fall asleep?"

"So, you'll stay all night?" His fingers creeped along the sheet as if he wanted to touch me but was trying to be subtle about it. "Please."

I planned to be at the hospital at ten and five, so I had no real reason to leave. Especially since he asked so nicely. "I will. As long as you're a good boy and drink all your milk."

His eyes lit up and he nodded excitedly. "I promise I will." He looked down at my chest and cocked his head. "Wait, what did you ask me before?"

It took me a second to get caught up with his line of thinking, and then I remembered where he'd veered off. "What position will be most comfortable for you to fall asleep?"

He scrunched his eyebrows and scooted lower on the bed. "I don't think I'll fall asleep at first, so...maybe just lying next to you. Will that be comfortable for you?"

"Yep." It was my preferred position in bed, but I didn't want to be presumptuous. I slipped my arm under his head to create a pillow so he was in alignment with my lower nipple and then let him go from there.

Ricky was much less tentative this time, quickly pressing his whole body against mine and then closing his lips over my nipple. His eyes fluttered shut with the first full pull, and I almost moaned out loud.

Fuck, that felt good.

I'd done this for clients and lovers regularly over the past ten years, and it was always nice. But between his pajamas, his innocence, and his eagerness...he just checked all my boxes.

And a few I didn't realize I had.

Like, the oral fixation.

I guess I assumed any guy I was with would be into my milk at some level...maybe occasionally during sex or for comfort, but Ricky seemed to love it. Not just as a novelty but as a human pacifier...which was fine with me.

Better than fine. It was fucking awesome.

As soon as he got into a steady rhythm of drinking, his hips began to slowly pulse against me, and I could feel his hard length poking me through his thin layer of cotton. I wanted nothing more than to reach into my shorts and stroke myself in time with his movements, but I didn't move an inch.

I let him control what happened next. Even when he reached behind himself and started tugging on the zipper.

After a few futile attempts, Ricky whined against me and opened his eyes without pulling off.

"You need help with that, baby?"

He nodded slightly and waited for me to reach back.

I tugged the zipper down over his round ass until it reached the apex of his thighs. "In the front too?"

He lifted his top leg up, so I could pull it from the front, right over his balls. *Sweet Jesus, he didn't make it easy to be a gentleman.*

Slowly, I moved my hand around his leg and lifted the tab that rested at his taint. I slipped my finger underneath the fabric to protect his skin and hair. When my finger grazed his balls, Ricky's hand curled into my side, digging his nails into my skin.

I almost came from that alone.

His hips started moving again, this time in slow motion, his length dragging along my thigh until the zipper released the fabric in front and his cock sprang free. Ricky took control from that moment, pulling off my lower side and sucking my upper nipple between his teeth before latching on and swallowing down a full gulp.

With a subtle shift of his body weight, he was fully on top of me, the bottoms of his feet pushing my calves together so he could fuck between my thighs, rubbing my balls through my shorts as his shallow strokes got faster and faster.

My breathing picked up at the same time that Ricky rolled my sensitive lower nipple between two fingers and then abruptly lifted his hips long enough to drop his blanket over my thighs so he could finish himself off by coming on his blanket instead of me or his sheets.

When his mouth opened wide to gasp against my skin as he came in a shuddering wave, I was almost disappointed that it didn't land on my skin.

I wanted to feel it on me. Wear his warmth. Taste him the way he tasted me.

But he just rocked against his blanket for a long moment as he rode out his orgasm and then licked the last drops of milk at my tip that had gathered after his abrupt release.

After a few seconds, Ricky slipped to the side of me and wadded up his blanket before tossing in on the ground. Then he rested his head on my biceps and looked up at me through hooded lids. "I'm ready to sleep now."

My throat was thick with lust and desire as he cuddled against me, his spent dick still exposed and resting against my leg. "Goodnight, sweet boy. Have happy dreams."

He smiled without opening his eyes. "My happiest one just came true."

11

RICKY

The problem with drinking so much milk at bedtime was having to go potty throughout the night. I had to get up twice—by myself—to pee. But it was easy since I was still unzipped.

I thought about zipping in, but I kinda liked being free while still dressed. It was…exciting. Exciting to know that Chad could see me…or touch me anytime he wanted.

Even though, so far, he didn't seem to want to.

That was okay. He was already doing a lot for me. What I needed to do was give something back to him. He didn't let me pay this time because it was a date, but I needed to do something to make him feel good too.

I couldn't just keep taking without giving.

And when I got back into bed just as the sun was starting to peek over the horizon, I knew exactly what that could be.

"My sweet boy." Chad was still mostly asleep as his arm wrapped around me, and he pulled me tightly on top of him. "Come to Daddy."

I was immediately hard again, just hearing him say that. Was he saying that to me or some other boy in his dreams? My heart was hoping he was dreaming about me, but whether or not he was, he was obviously having a happy dream.

Which gave me the opportunity I'd been waiting for.

I shifted my weight so I could slide my hand down his stomach and to the edge of his boxers. It took a minute for me to find the courage to go for it, but once I did, I really did. I slipped my fingers under the fabric and immediately came into contact with his hard cock.

It jumped under my fingertips, but when I flattened my hand over his full length, his hips rolled up, instinctively looking for more. And I was happy to provide it.

My thumb traced the top of his head as my fingers circled his hard shaft and gave a small tug.

"Yes, baby. Like that." Chad's low voice surprised me, but I wasn't sure if he was awake or asleep. What I did know was that he enjoyed what I was doing, so I kept it up, stroking him faster and moving in rhythm with the rocking motion he was making.

When I couldn't resist any longer, I scooted down and pushed his shorts lower so I could take him into my mouth.

It had been a few years since I'd given a blow job, but it was like riding a bike. And I was excellent at riding bikes. My jaw quickly remembered how to relax enough to create a warm tunnel without any pesky teeth getting in the way. And when he finally came in my mouth, I swallowed every drop, loving the contrast in taste from whatI was used to from Chad's sweet milk.

He could feed me anything and I'd love it.

If I didn't check myself, I was gonna start to love him…and I wasn't sure either of us were ready for that. But I really wanted to be.

"That was a nice surprise, sweet boy." Chad was fully awake now as his fingers combed through my hair and then gently tugged it so I was looking at him. "Can I get a kiss up here too?"

God, yes! I scrambled up him and pressed my lips to his, sharing what was left of his flavor when my tongue swiped over his.

"Mmm, you taste…happy." He cupped my cheek, giving me a place to rest as I looked into his eyes.

"I am…cause you know why?" I was in the fuzzy stage between big and little, coherent enough to have a big conversation but not interested in all the big words. "Cause you called me sweet boy. And in your dream, you said you're sweet boy's Daddy. So, that's me, right?"

Chad grinned as he wrapped his other arm around my back and held me even tighter. "You're the sweetest boy I know. And the only one I want in my arms. So, yeah, it's definitely you."

My head fell forward, landing on his chin as I basked in the moment.

He wanted me. And I wanted him.

"C'mere, baby." He lifted my chin so I was facing him and then kissed me again, pulling me into a bliss I'd never felt before.

Every place he touched me burned like fire, branding me with a claim I wanted the whole world to see. But more than that, I wanted to hear him call me his sweet boy when he was awake and really meant it.

"Sorry I woke you up." I kissed him again, and when his hand slipped around my hip and cupped my balls, I almost squealed right in his mouth.

"Can I help take care of this?" His fingers lightly closed around my cock, and I almost fainted.

"Yes, Daddy."

His breath hitched as he licked over my lips and began to gently stroke me.

Nipping his chin, I thrust into his fist. After a few seconds, I moved my legs over his so he could still reach me while I could reach his chest and latch on. It was what we both needed.

I milked Chad's chest while he milked my cock. And when we'd both swallowed up as much as we could from each other, he pulled me back up onto his body and we fell asleep again, getting a few more hours of rest before the warmth of the sun heated the room to the point that we were both ready to get up.

12

CHAD

I didn't want to wake up. If I could've stayed in that bed with Ricky for the rest of my life, I would have. But we were both covered in a light sheen of sweat, and my body was sore from being in the same position all night long. I needed to move.

"Good morning."

Surprised he was awake, I looked down at Ricky and smiled. "Good morning, sweet boy. Are you ready to get up?"

"Not really, but I guess we have to." He yawned and lifted one arm, stretching with a twist and arching his back like a sleepy kitten. "I think I need a shower."

Excellent idea. "Me too. How do you feel about conserving water and taking one together?"

He smiled widely and nodded. "Yeah. I like saving water."

I patted his bottom gently and glanced toward the bathroom door. "Hop up, sweetheart. I might have time for breakfast before I've got to get to work."

His lower lip jutted out when I mentioned leaving for work. "You have to go?" He got out of bed, still unzipped from ass up and around to his bellybutton, but he didn't try to cover himself. *Good boy.*

"Yeah, in about an hour. I wish I could stay longer, but I have to see clients this morning."

His shoulders dropped, and he turned to me, this time dropping his hands over his dick as if hiding it from me. "Clients that you have to see in person?"

His face was absolutely devastated, and I wasn't sure where things had suddenly gone so wrong. "Yes, but only for a few hours. What's wrong?"

Ricky's lower lip started to tremble, and he turned away, rushing into the bathroom. "Nothing."

Wrong answer, baby. "Ricky, turn around."

His whole body went rigid, and then he turned to me with big eyes.

"Last night, we talked about you being my sweet boy, right?"

That full lip began to quiver again as he slowly nodded.

"And do sweet boys lie to their Daddy?"

A single tear slipped from his eye as he slowly moved his head from left to right. "No," he whispered.

I placed my hand on this cheek and used my thumb to wipe away the tear before leaning forward and kissing his forehead. "Then you will always tell me the truth. Do you understand?"

He sniffled before blowing out a deep sigh. "Yes, Daddy."

Fuck, I liked how that sounded. What I didn't like was seeing the hurt in his eyes and hearing the pain in his voice. Tilting his head up so he was looking right at me, I took a step back and stared right at him. "Okay, then let's try this again. Why are you so sad right now?"

His chin fell forward so I was looking at the top of his head, not his anguished eyes. "I guess I'm sad that you have to go to work but more sad that you're seeing a client. I wish I could be your only client."

"Oh." I'd never had a relationship where my partner was jealous of my business. Seeing clients was just something I'd done for so long that it never played a part in my personal life. But I wanted my relationship with Ricky to be different, and I was willing to work to make that happen. Wanting to hash things out before we got in the shower, I slipped one arm behind his back and the other behind his knees and lifted him into the air.

Ricky instinctively circled his arms around my neck and relaxed, resting his head on my shoulder as I took the few steps back to his bed and sat down.

"Thank you for being honest with me. I can see how an exclusive relationship would include you being the exclusive one to feed from me." I thought about that for a moment as I considered my current client list. "Let me first tell you that I don't have a sexual relationship with my clients. As you know from the first time I was here, when I'm being paid, I don't touch or do anything inappropriate."

He bit his lip as if he wanted to say what I knew was on his mind, but he held his breath, allowing me to continue.

"But, as you also know, sometimes the client can take things a bit further on their own, and I understand that's a boundary you're not comfortable with me crossing."

Ricky sucked in a deep breath and his lip pushed out again. "I can be comfortable with it. I know you can't change everything just for me. So as long as I get you at bedtime, I can share."

I didn't want him to feel like he had to share me or that he was settling for only a portion of what he deserved. Ricky deserved every bit of me if that was what he wanted. But I did have some commitments I had to take care of before I could make major changes in my client list. "The clients I'm seeing today are newborn babies."

Ricky's eyes went wide and his jaw fell open. "Like real babies?"

"Yep. In the intensive care unit at the hospital. They were born early and don't have a mom who can feed them, so I've been hired to feed them twice a day while they're supplemented with formula and to hold them. We call it skin-to-skin therapy, and it's important for their development in these early days."

He smiled, finally relaxing. "That's so sweet. I love babies."

I cocked my head, quickly veering from my original plan. "Would you like to come with me today? After I feed them, I usually just hold them for an hour or two. You can help."

Ricky's eyes got big as he realized what I was saying. "You mean, I might be able to hold one of the tiny babies?"

"Yep." I kissed the tip of his nose, so happy that he was feeling better about the day. "Let's get all cleaned up, and I'll let my friend at the hospital know that he's got two helpers for today."

Ricky threw his arms around my neck and kissed me hard, smashing his lips to mine and claiming me like I'd just given him an engagement ring. "You're the best Daddy ever. I'm sorry I was being selfish. I want you to help little babies get strong and healthy."

I closed my arms around him tight, glad he understood where I was coming from. I pulled back and stared into his eyes. "If we're gonna do this—be in a relationship—we're gonna be exclusive. I'm only *your* Daddy and you're only *my* boy. No one else has any part of us in that way. Which means, I'll need to reevaluate my business model."

Ricky sighed and held up his hand to stop me from going on. "No, it's okay, Chad. You can still see your clients. I don't want to be greedy, and I love that you want to help people."

He was such a sweet boy.

"I have enough business from the frozen and fresh milk deliveries that I don't need to take on private clients. And if you're fine with occasional requests from the hospital for babies in need, I'll refer my adult clients to other consultants I know. There are plenty of us to go around." I shrugged and made sure he knew how sincere I was by holding both of his cheeks steady. "I was just trying to stay busy until I found you."

I leaned forward and pressed my lips to his, soaking up his warmth and affection in a way that gave new meaning to skin-on-skin contact.

This thing between us was moving at light speed, but it didn't feel rushed or sudden.

It felt perfect.

13

RICKY

Over the next few weeks, things were great.

Chad was able to transfer all his in-person clients to his colleagues from the local branch of The Lactin Brotherhood, and the babies were finally being discharged from the hospital. A nice family was eager to adopt them, and we were both happy to know they would be loved and well taken care of.

Things for me had been a little crazy at work. While Chad was able to adjust his schedule to work for the needs and timing requirements of our new relationship, I didn't have that same luxury. I still had to go into an office every day and deal with complicated clients and an even more complicated team of drama seekers.

At least, the project with the medspa had been wrapped up. And since I was able to help recover over two million dollars from the ring of managers who had been embezzling from the company, I got a 5% bonus. And after discussing the best way to spend it with Chad, I decided to put all that money straight into the bank.

But the real fun I had was when I got to help Chad with his business.

He let me take over the bookkeeping and billing because those were the least fun parts of the job for him. Fortunately, they were the most fun parts for me. I was able to not only find some new contracts for him through my own client contacts, but he'd also been approved as a vendor to several organizations within our county to provide milk to women with babies and children.

On the days I got to go with him to make those deliveries, I was so proud that he was my Daddy. Of course, I was proud of him every day, but I felt ten feet tall when I saw and felt the gratitude from all the moms who needed help keeping their children fed and healthy.

A BORN PROVIDER

It was a feeling I had never felt before, and I wanted to do even more to help others.

I had a few ideas for ways I could work with some of Chad's friends from The Lactin Brotherhood to not only help them build their businesses but to also make positive changes in the world.

But tonight wasn't a night for those kinds of ideas.

I had a much more important idea to run past my Daddy when he got home from the gym. Well, my home. He spent the weekend nights with me so I could wake up with him, but he was pumping even more often now that it was his whole business model, so on work days, he was usually at his house until the evening when he came over for dinner and stayed until I fell asleep.

Getting cuddled and falling asleep with a real live pacifier in my mouth was the best feeling in the world. Waking up alone wasn't, and that was why I couldn't hold in my idea any longer.

The slow cooker had been cooking lemon chicken all day, and I made a pot of pasta to eat with it so when Chad got back, I didn't have to fuss in the kitchen.

As soon as I heard the door open, I ran to him and leaped into his arms, holding on tightly. I was always so happy to see him after spending the whole day apart.

In the short time we'd been together, my need to be around him had only increased.

I thought maybe we would start wanting some space by now, but neither of us ever wanted to be apart for more than a few hours at a time. On the days when I had the chance to work at home, I begged him to hang out with me for as long as possible because I just liked knowing he was there.

Chad wrapped his arms around me and kissed me hard before pressing his forehead to mine. "Damn, baby. I love when you greet me like this." His arms squeezed a little tighter and he kissed along my jaw to my earlobe. "I love you."

My heart started beating faster as I pulled back and looked him right in the eyes. "Did you just say what I think you said?"

He chuckled and cocked his head to the side. "If you think I just said that I love you, then, yes, I did."

A BORN PROVIDER

My mouth smashed his, kissing him deeply as I rubbed my erection against his washboard abs. "I love you too, Daddy. And I love that you love me."

Chad chuckled again, blowing warm air into my mouth. "You know what else I love?"

His palms squeezed my bottom, so I thought that was what he was gonna say. He didn't spend a lot of time around my bottom. I'd tried my best to make it clear that I wanted to have sex like that, but so far, he'd been taking it slow.

Just hands and mouths.

And our hands and mouths all felt so good, I had no complaints.

Even though I really wanted to feel him inside me.

"What else do you love?" I looked up at him, hanging on every word.

"Whatever smells so good. It's making my stomach growl. What did you make?"

"Oh, I made you dinner." I slid down his body and reached for his hand. "Do you need to shower or change or do anything before we eat?"

He dropped his bag by the couch and slipped off his shoes. "No, I showered at the gym, so I'm all yours."

Closing my eyes, I took a deep breath and relished those words. I loved every time he said he was all mine.

I knew the way he meant it was in the context of our evening, but I really believed he meant it in every other context too.

Especially now that he loved me.

14

CHAD

Dinner was delicious. Ricky didn't usually make elaborate dinners, but he could follow a recipe, and when he wanted to get fancy, he nailed it. And throughout the entire meal, I could sense there was something weighing on him.

Now that I didn't have to go to the hospital twice a day, I toyed with the idea of staying over more often, but I wasn't sure if it was too soon to make that kind of suggestion. And then Ricky beat me to the punch.

When he was done eating, he scooted back from his little table and clasped his hands in his lap. "I have an idea."

"Okay, hit me." I took a drink of water and leaned back

in my chair, fully focused on him even though I'd just loaded my plate with a third serving.

"Well, I don't like when you're not here in the morning…"

"I don't like it either." At least he and I were on the same page on that. Not that he'd made any secret of his likes and dislikes…

"So, maybe, since you don't like it and I don't like it… you can just live here. With me. All the time."

I grinned and reached across the table to hold his hand. "That's a great idea, but are you sure you're ready for that? It's a big step, and we haven't been together for that long."

"It's long enough to do everything!" He was a bit more forceful than usual but then inhaled a calming breath and blew it out slowly. "I mean, yes, I'm ready for that and everything. I'm ready, Chad." He looked me right in the eyes, using my name to make sure I knew he was in a grown-up headspace and not being bratty.

He was ready.

"I'm ready too, sweetheart." I stood up and went to him, tugging him to his feet so I could hold him. "I love you, and I would love to live here with you."

"Really?" He bit his lip, reining in his excitement. "What about the other stuff?"

I knew what he was talking about, and I was tired of waiting too. "You mean sex?"

He swallowed hard as he nodded. "Yeah, the real kind."

I grinned. "I think we're ready for that too… What do you think?"

"Yes!" He slipped his arms up around my neck and pulled me in for a sloppy kiss. "We're so ready."

Chuckling, I looked down at the table. "If you're done eating, I'll get this cleaned up and we can watch a movie in bed."

"Okay." He kissed me again and then pulled away. "I'm gonna take a shower and pick a movie."

By the time Ricky got out of the shower, I was naked and under the covers, already comfortable on my side of the bed. Or what I had claimed as my side of the bed on my very first visit here.

And since I'd just agreed to move in, I planned to

spend a lot of time right here…for as long as he'd have me.

Ricky was wrapped in a towel, but instead of getting dressed, he tossed the towel onto the chair and slipped into the bed fully naked.

"You're so beautiful." I never got tired of looking at his slim body with hints of muscles but plenty of softness. "Come here, sweet boy."

"One sec." Before climbing onto me, he turned to his nightstand and pulled out a strip of condoms and a bottle of lube. Then he curled into my side, throwing one leg over my hip and his arm over my chest. "Just in case."

I kissed the top of his head and gave him a squeeze as my arm held him in place. "It's good to be prepared."

He nodded but kept his head down. "Yeah, I'm all the way prepared. Just in case."

Grinning, I reached for the remote and turned on the TV. "So, what movie did you pick?"

His hand slipped up my chest and cupped the muscle, kneading it lightly. "Maybe Fifty Shades."

Well, shit. He was really going for it, wasn't he? "Have you seen it before?"

Ricky nodded and peeked up. "Yeah, have you?"

"Mmm-hmm." I pulled up the streaming app and found the movie.

For a full forty minutes, we sat quietly and watched the movie, not doing anything to increase the building tension between us. But once the first sexy scene came on, we were both hard and ready, no longer pretending we could keep it cool.

Ricky climbed over my body and rubbed his erection on my leg as his lips found mine. "You smell so good, Daddy." When his hand wrapped around my cock and gave it a nice tug, I knew I was done.

My palms closed on his sides, starting just under his armpits and slowly sliding down his body until I was cupping his ass cheeks, kneading the warm flesh and gently pulling it apart with my fingertips. Teasing his hole, my finger easily slipped inside his opening. He was already lubed up and loosened for me.

Ricky moaned and pushed harder against me as he scooted higher so I was in line with his opening. He pulled his lips away from mine long enough to ask for permission to get me ready too. "May I?"

"Of course, baby. I'm all yours." I lifted my hand to his cheek and gently cupped him as I leaned forward and kissed his mouth one more time. "In every way. Take what you need."

He squirmed over my knees as he carefully rolled the condom onto my cock and covered me with lube. Then, he reached behind himself and added some more before lifting up and placing his hole right at the tip of my ready dick.

I grinned at his assertiveness. "If I had known you were this eager, we would've done this a long time ago."

Surprising both of us, he dropped down hard, pushing me all the way inside his channel with a groan as our sounds filled the room.

I held his hips in place, needing a second to compose myself. "Fuck, boy. You're so tight."

He shivered and closed his eyes as he sucked in slow breaths for a moment before looking at me again. "I've been ready for a long time. Don't make me wait again."

"Never."

I never expected Ricky to be so aggressive in the bedroom, but I fucking loved it. I loved that he not only knew what he wanted but was willing to take it.

From me. He wanted it from me and was taking it from me. His Daddy.

"You ready, baby?" I looked into his eyes and waited for him to meet my gaze.

He nodded. "I'm ready, Daddy. Make me feel good."

15

RICKY

When I finally got to feel Chad inside me, I knew that we were meant to be.

We had both waited for love for so long, and it was clear that we had been waiting for each other.

No one else could make me melt with just a look.

Quiver with just a touch.

Or be completely filled up with warmth from a single drink.

He knew how to take care of me when I needed it, but also how to let me take charge when I was ready to do that.

And apparently, when it came to finally having sex, I was ready to be in charge. At least in the beginning. Now, I wasn't sure I could move with all the big feelings and intense energy flowing through me.

Chad's firm grip guided me up and down his length several times, rubbing all the right spots as I gripped my own cock. I put my left hand over his chest and gave him a gentle squeeze, shocked when a spray of milk came out and splashed against my stomach.

A full-body shutter rocked through me, and I almost came just from that. But I held my breath and rode it out a little bit longer.

I didn't want to finish before Daddy did, but it all just felt so amazing.

"You're such a good boy, Ricky. You make Daddy feel so good." His strokes became faster, deeper, as he plowed up into me.

I was breathless as I moaned. "I'm so close."

Chad's pace became faster and his breath more labored as he moved in and out of me. After a few minutes, his hand replaced mine and the other slipped around my waist, anchoring me in place against him.

Stroking my cock with one hand, he thrust into me with firm motions.

I couldn't hold back any longer. "I'm coming, Daddy. It's too much."

It was too much and not enough…and everything.

With my head thrown back and facing the ceiling, I came hard, spraying Daddy's chest as he grunted through his own orgasm, with me tightening around him.

The aftershocks of my climax continued for a long time, but when I finally lifted off his dick and landed on his chest, my mouth immediately went to his nipple. I could taste myself on his salty skin, but that was quickly washed away with the sweet warmth that filled my mouth and made me sleepy.

We both needed to get up, but I couldn't imagine moving anywhere quite yet.

"You doing okay, sweet boy?" Chad slid his hand up and down my spine, gently rounding his palm over my tender bottom.

"Mmm-hmm." I moaned against his skin without pulling off, not wanting to release him just yet.

His fingers combed through my hair, and his arms closed over my back, keeping me warm against his heated muscles. "Have your snack, sweetheart, and then we'll get you in the bath."

That sounded like heaven.

"And then we'll talk about what I need to pack so I can stay here with you all the time."

Daddy used the softest towel I owned to gently wash my body, making sure to get my dick extra clean because he said he might need to kiss it later. That made it hard, which made the scrubbing feel too good…so I made my bathwater dirty and had to finish with a shower.

That worked out to my benefit because Daddy climbed in with me and we were able to wash each other.

When we went to sleep, I put on one of the new special zipper pajamas I'd been collecting. That way, if Daddy did want to kiss any part of me, he wouldn't have trouble getting to it.

And then I found my blankie under my pillow and waited for Daddy to turn off the lights and climb in beside me.

"You're really gonna move in with me? Like, stay here forever?"

He chuckled and kissed my forehead. "Um, yes, I would love to move in. The lease on my place isn't up for a few more months, so if there are any issues or you need some space sometimes, I can always go back there. And if not, I'll fully move out by the end of the year."

"I won't need space." I licked across his nipple and then blew on it, making it harden before I did it again. "I want you here forever."

He shuddered and pulled my hand up to his other nipple, silently hinting it needed some attention too. "Me too, baby. But let's start with the rest of this month and go from there."

I couldn't resist closing my lips over him and taking a strong pull, filling my mouth with his warm milk. It was so delicious, and I always felt so sleepy when I drank from him. "Starting tonight?"

His strong hand gripped my neck, holding me against him. "I'll pick up everything I need tomorrow and can slowly move things over."

I took another pull and then looked up at him. "I love you, Daddy. Thank you for loving me too."

"I love you too, sweet boy. Now finish your milk and get to sleep. I'll be right here when you wake. Tomorrow and every day after."

More from The Lactin Brotherhood...

- Male lactation to reward his boy

- Jock who needs some discipline

- First-time male lactation

- College roommates turned lovers

- **Order Now**

- Male lactation starting in mid-thirties

- Experienced little ready to help

- An oral fixation

- Low angst sweetness

- **<u>Order Now</u>**

- Male lactation that started as a child but becomes a problem at forty

- Experienced little who lusts for milk

- First time Daddy, finding his stride

- Low angst sweetness

- **<u>Order Now</u>**

- Male lactation for comfort

- Sweet first-time Daddy

- Experienced little who loves milk at bedtime

- All the low-angst cuteness you can handle

<u>Order Now</u>

Are you a writer or an aspiring writer?

If you have an idea for a Lactin Brotherhood book and would like to co-write with Alex or write your own book in this universe, please request information at TheLactinBrotherhood.com or sign up here https://forms.gle/1CZ1JMpcjkypZtyH9

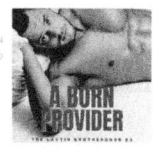

Made in the USA
Coppell, TX
27 February 2025